Rip van Winkle

Original story by Washington Irving

Retold by Kay Brown

Illustrated by Gerry Embleton

DERRYDALE
A division of Crown Publishers, Inc.
New York

© Award Publications Ltd. MCMLXXVIII
Spring House, Spring Place
London NW5, England.
Library of Congress Catalog Card Number : LOC 79-51468
All rights reserved
This edition is published by Derrydale, a division
of Crown Publishers, Inc., One Park Avenue
New York, New York 10016
a b c d e f g h
Printed in Belgium.

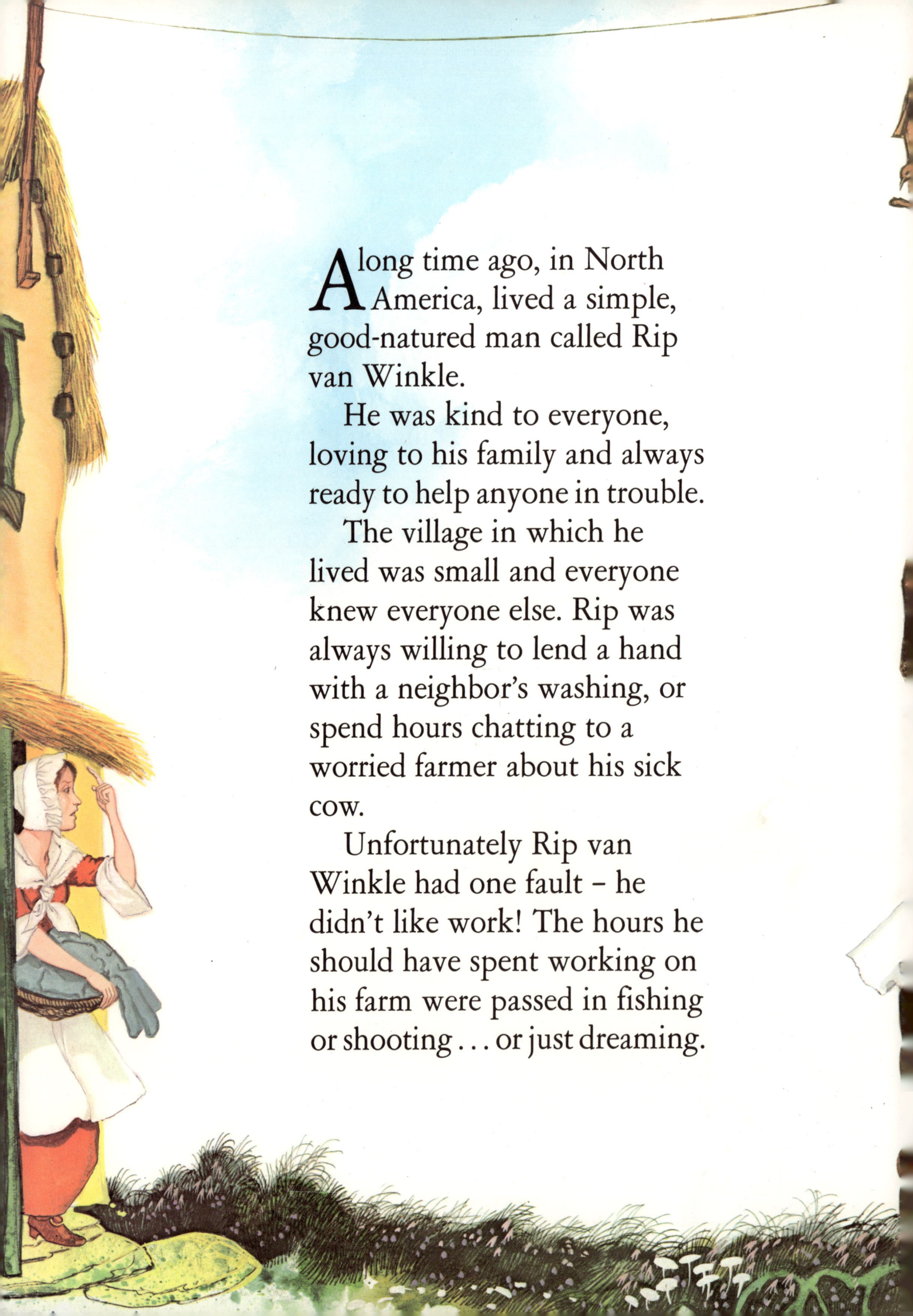

A long time ago, in North America, lived a simple, good-natured man called Rip van Winkle.

He was kind to everyone, loving to his family and always ready to help anyone in trouble.

The village in which he lived was small and everyone knew everyone else. Rip was always willing to lend a hand with a neighbor's washing, or spend hours chatting to a worried farmer about his sick cow.

Unfortunately Rip van Winkle had one fault – he didn't like work! The hours he should have spent working on his farm were passed in fishing or shooting... or just dreaming.

But Rip's favorite escape was to take his
gun and climb slowly into the mountains. He
didn't mind if there was nothing to shoot at; he
liked to find new and different paths across the
slopes and then to settle on a grassy bank,
stretch out among the flowers, stare at the
misty mountain tops and dream.

One day, on one such long walk, Rip saw in
the distance a small man with a tall hat and
flapping coat, bent almost double under the
weight of a barrel.

the Royal George

Fine Ale

At other times, if he could escape quietly from the house while his wife was busy, he would go to the local inn to meet his friends. Here, sitting in the sunshine, they would talk for hours and tell each other long, sleepy stories. Often these were about the mountains surrounding the village, the Catskills, which reached far into the clouds and seemed to change color from day to day. Many of the villagers thought these mysterious mountains held magical secrets; none of Rip's friends had ever ventured beyond the lower slopes, but what they didn't know they invented and the tales of the mountains grew wilder and more imaginative week by week!

Poor Rip van Winkle, as often as not, would be in the middle of listening to one such story and sipping his frothing beer, when his bullying wife would burst in, broom in hand, to chase him home to the housework. Rip hardly ever heard the endings to his friends' stories!

The children loved him
best, though, for he always
had time to fly their kites,
play endless games of marbles
or, most popular of all, tell
stories of ghosts, witches and
Indians. And if his wife was
heard raging through the
village in search of her
husband, there was always
someone who warned Rip
to hide before she found
him out!

Rip went to live with his daughter and her family and his adventure soon became known to everyone in the village. The children he had played marbles with long ago brought their children to hear him talk of the tall mountains, the strange, silent people he saw there and the magic barrel from which he drank.

He told his story to every stranger that came to the village, although some smiled to themselves as though they didn't believe him. Just the same, no-one was anxious to venture onto the Catskill mountains after dark and every time thunder is heard on the mountain slopes, the villagers wonder to this day if the eight strange little men are again playing bowls.

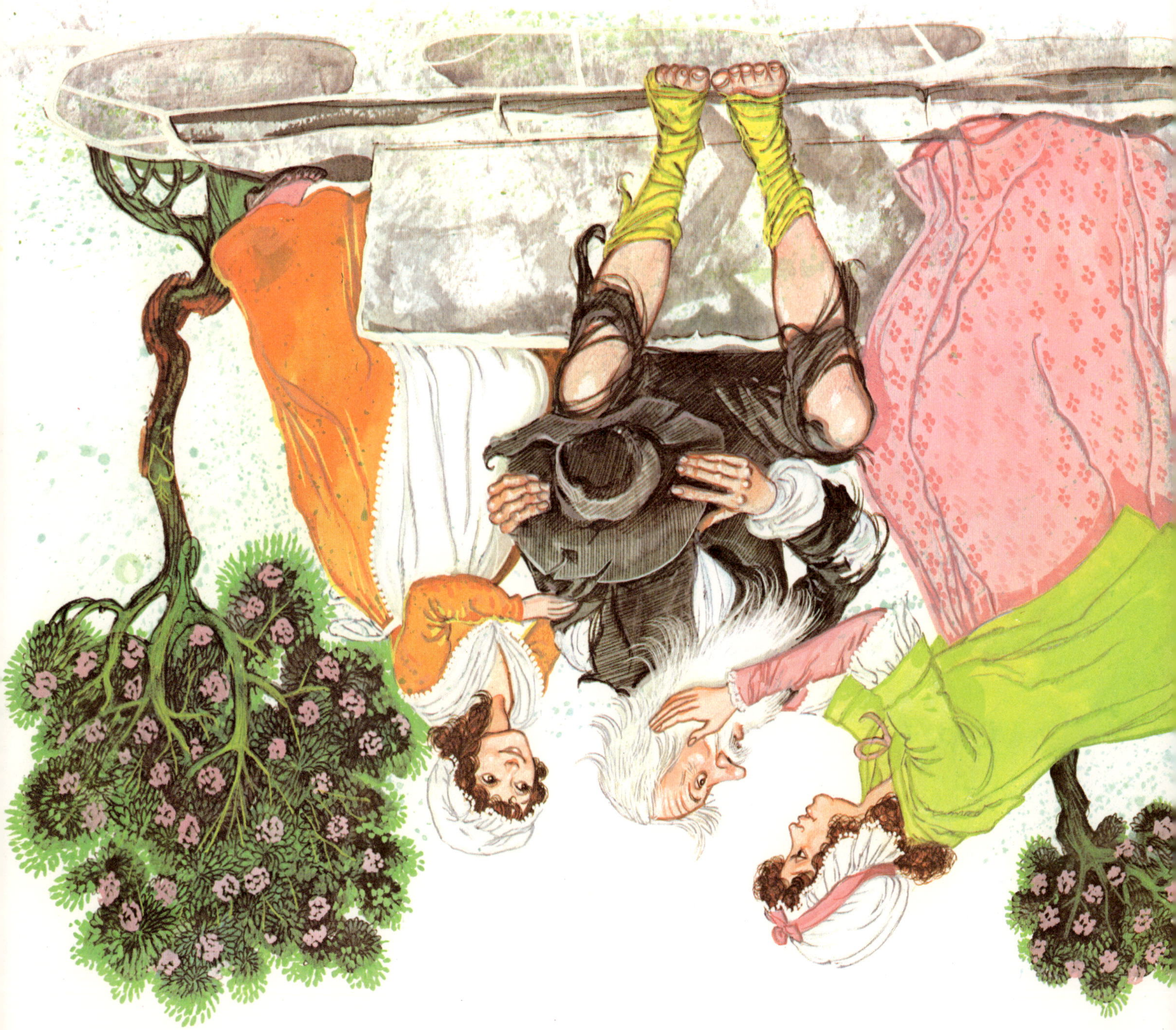

Rip made his way even more slowly and miserably down the street. He couldn't understand what had happened to him that night on the mountain, but he was sure of one thing: he was now twenty years older and no-one, it seemed, remembered him. He was wondering what to do next when he noticed a friendly old fellow with thick spectacles staring hard at him. "Surely" the fellow muttered "It *can't* be? Not after all this time . . . it is! Rip van Winkle, my old friend!" It was one of the group who had long ago shared stories and ale at "The Royal George."

Rip told him of his strange adventure and asked for news of his wife and daughter. His old friend explained that Rip's wife had died several years before, but his daughter had grown up, married and now had a daughter of her own. "Wait here and I'll tell her the good news" he said. Soon Rip was re-united with his daughter and, laughing and crying, again recounted his tale of the man he had met on the mountain.

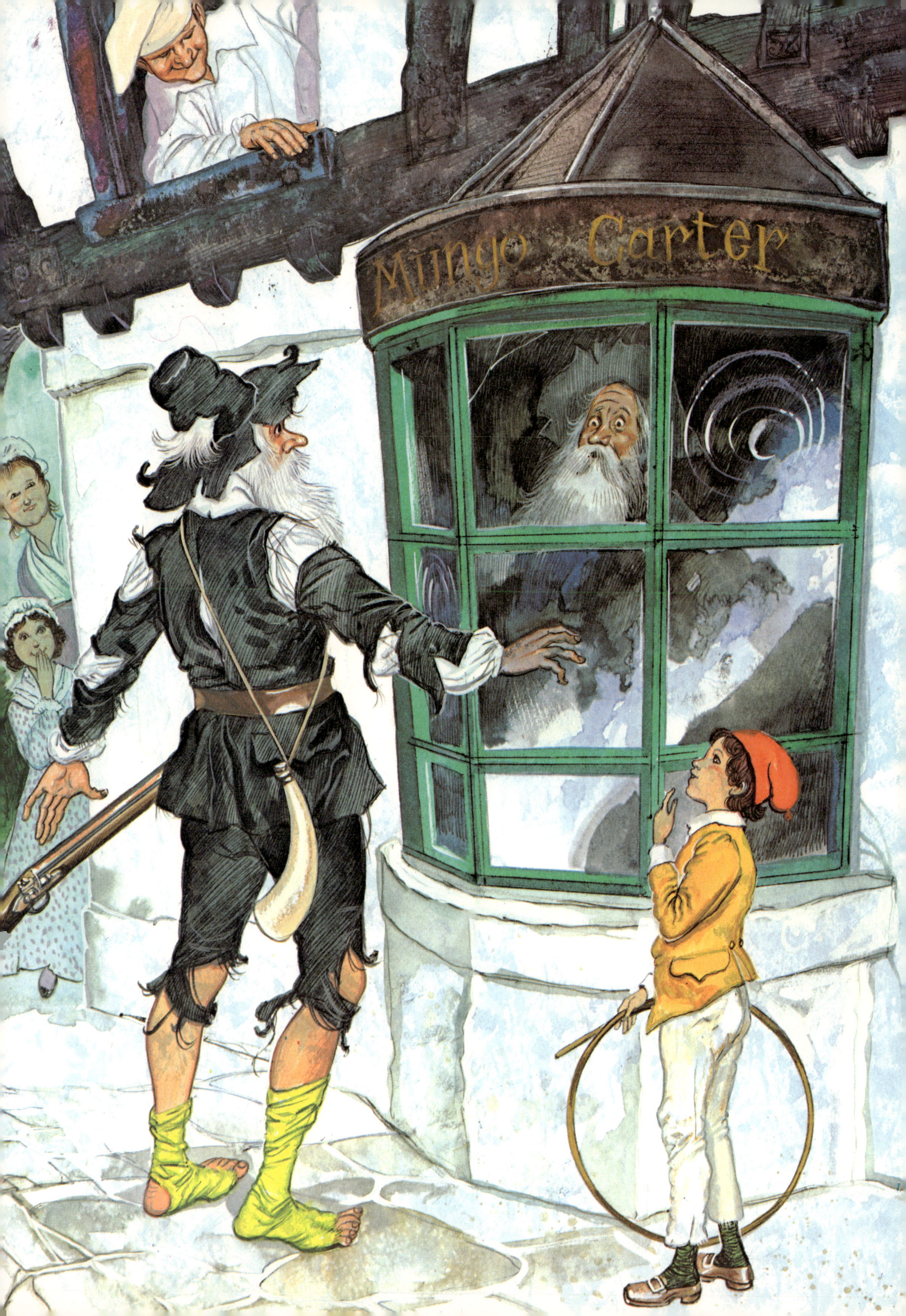
Mungo Carter

His wife was known to have a terrible temper: she didn't seem to see the kindly side of her husband's nature and nagged and bullied him at every opportunity.

"You never lift a finger at home" she complained "Yet you're always ready to help anyone else!"

Rip was never heard to complain, but all the village people felt sorry for him. Whenever he went for a walk he was greeted by friendly, sympathetic smiles. Even the dogs knew he was their friend and not one ever barked at him.

After walking in silence for some time Rip and the strange little man arrived at a level clearing. There, to Rip's great surprise, were seven other small, oddly-dressed people, playing a game which looked like bowls. But none of them smiled or spoke: instead they stared at Rip until his heart thumped and his knees trembled.

Rip was so surprised to see anyone else on the mountain that he watched the stranger for a while from behind a rock. He was certainly dressed most peculiarly and had a long and bushy beard. But, after a while, Rip's kind nature got the better of him and he called to the old man, asking if he would like some help. The stranger said nothing, but held out the heavy barrel, staring at Rip oddly. As Rip took the barrel and lifted it to his shoulder he heard a sound like thunder in the distance. He felt rather uneasy with the stranger close behind him, but went the way he was shown.

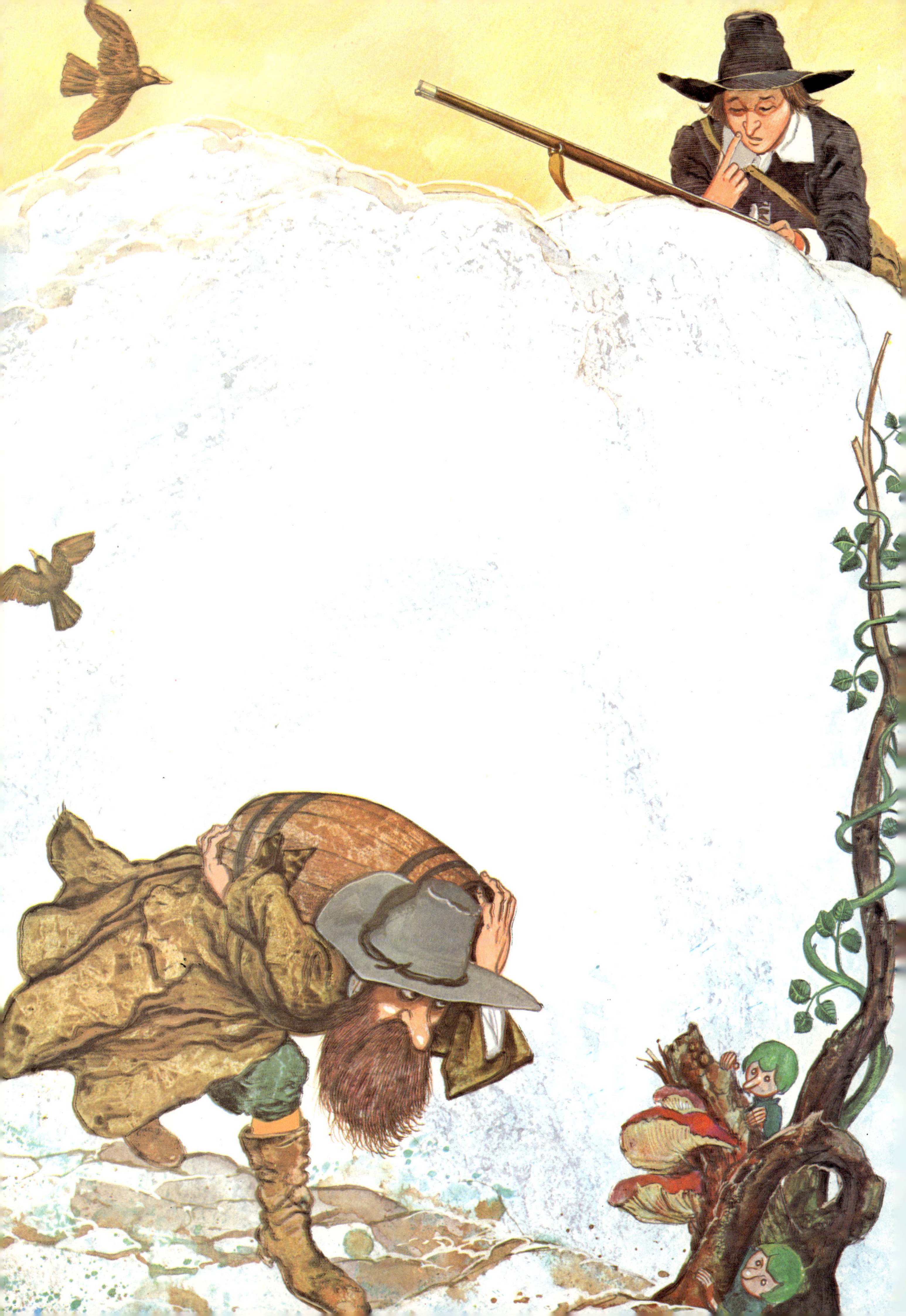

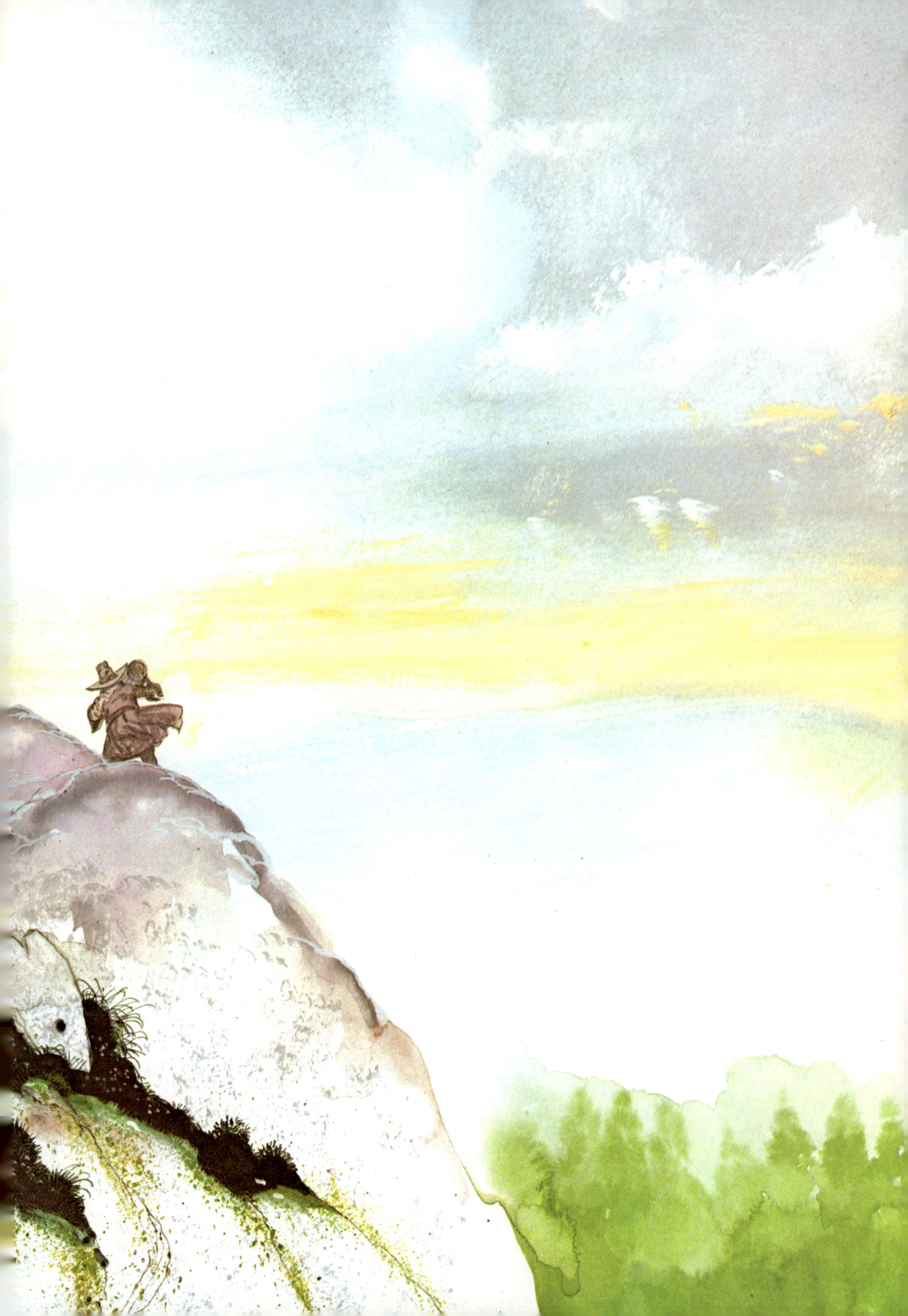

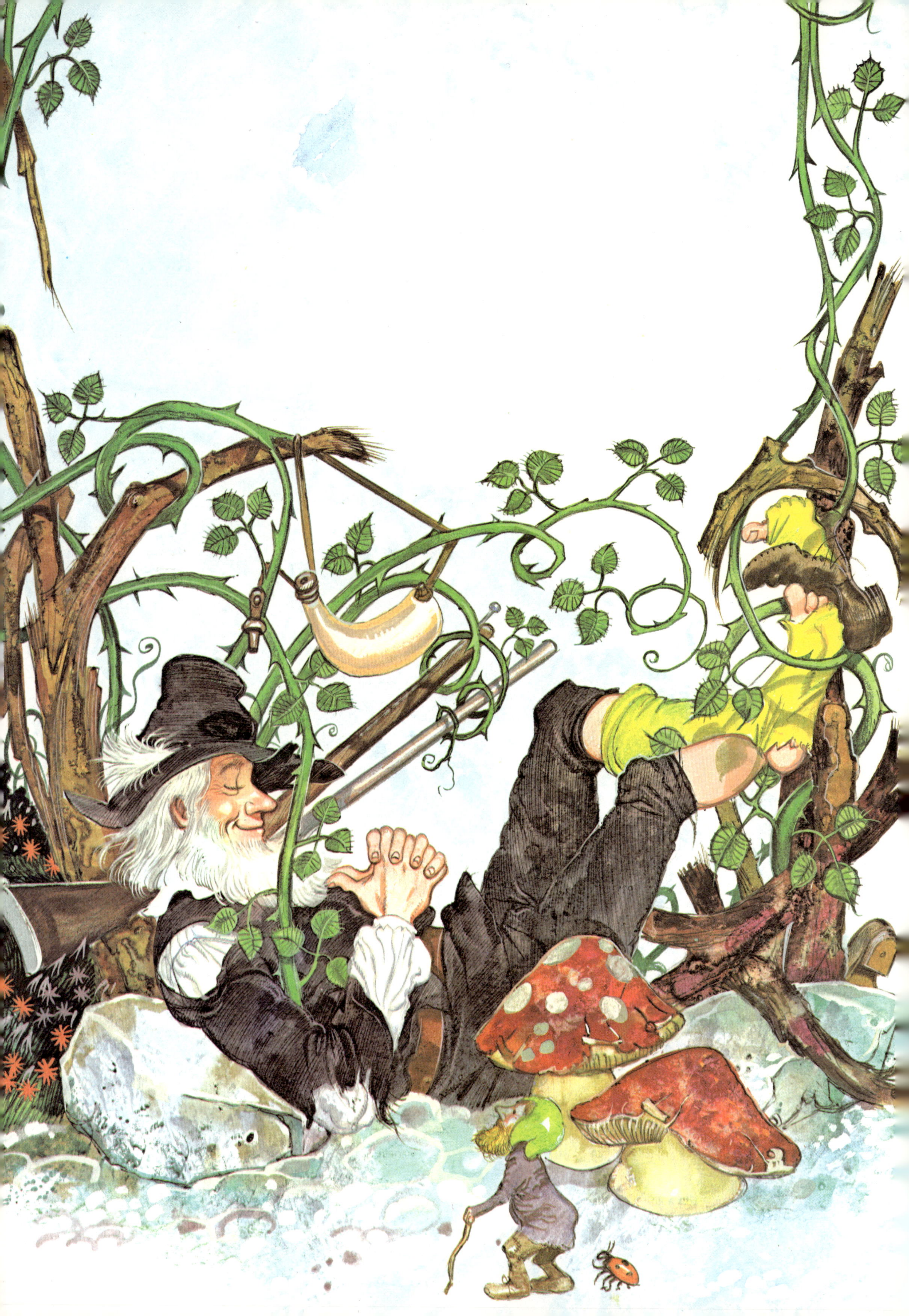

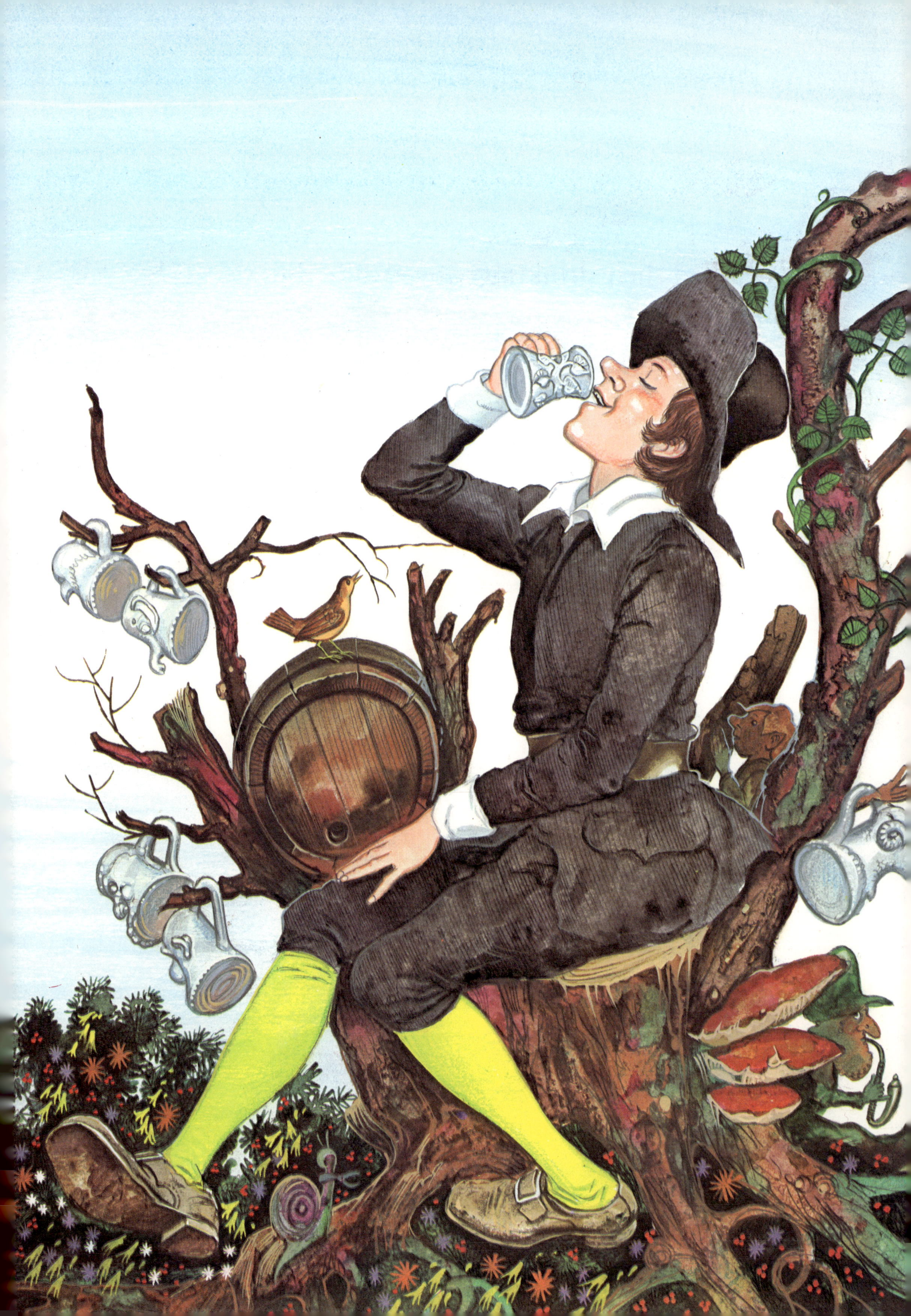

The strangers took the barrel from him and filled their drinking cups. While they drank they carried on with the game, all the time without speaking a word. It was as if Rip wasn't there! Soon Rip's curiosity – and his thirst – made him brave enough to try some of the liquid from the barrel. It was very good, even better than the innkeeper's frothy beer! No-one seemed to have noticed him, so he filled his cup again . . . and again.

After a while the little men did stop their game and watched him, but by this time Rip's eyes were shut and he was feeling very relaxed and very, very drowsy.

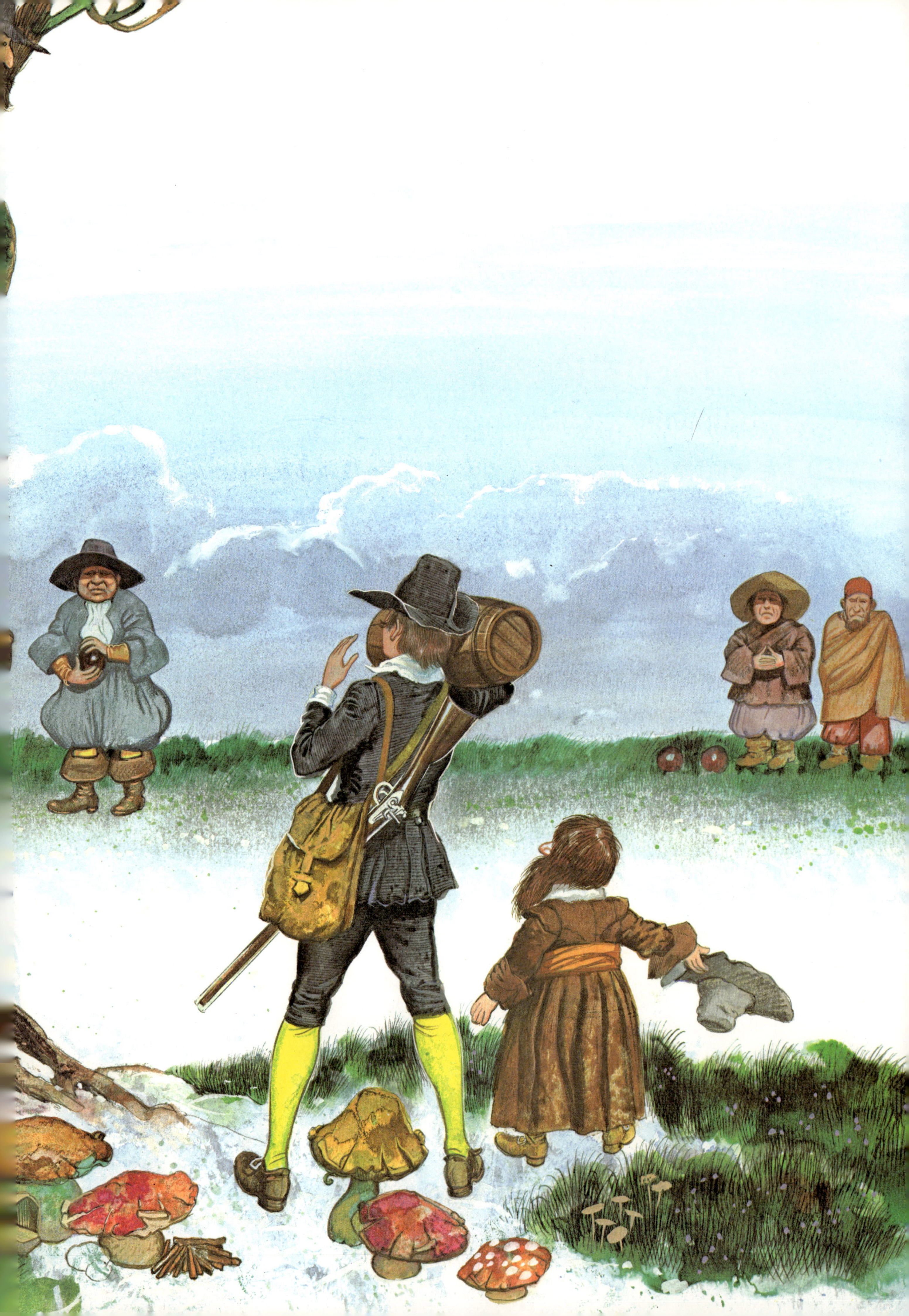

When Rip awoke, he was amazed to find himself on the same grassy bank where he had first seen the old man with the barrel. He sat up, very slowly – for his legs and back were stiff and aching. It was a bright, sunny morning: Rip looked around him for signs of the little people but he was quite alone. He tried to move his arms and legs . . . but they were caught up in a thorny bush! His jacket and trousers were torn and tattered and his shoes, his *best* shoes, were in shreds! Rip reached for his gun: the barrel, which he had spent many hours polishing, was thick with rust and fell in two in his hands.

Gradually he remembered the barrel and his drinking from it. "Oh that drink, that wicked drink!" thought Rip. "Whatever shall I tell my wife?"

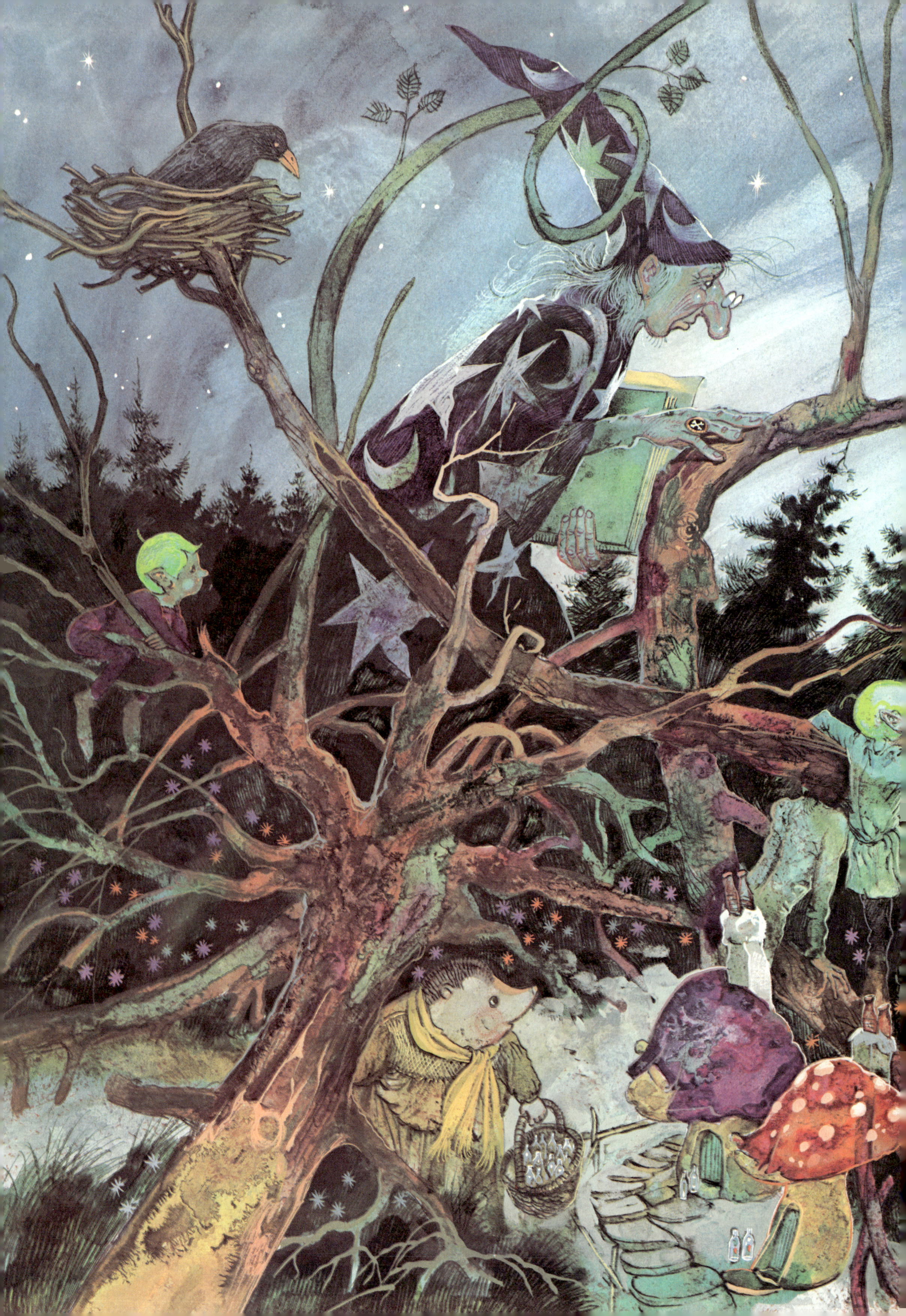

When he reached the village next morning it was busy with people – but all were dressed in clothes he didn't recognize. He looked eagerly for a face he knew – a storyteller from the inn, perhaps, or one of the children. But he knew no-one, and no-one knew him!

He got slowly to his feet and began to walk down the mountain. But everything seemed different: there were streams where paths had been and the undergrowth was thicker and wilder. His body ached and his feet were sore; night was falling before he came to the foot of the mountain and could see the village below him. Rip was so tired he could go no further: he crawled miserably under a bush and slept until morning.

As Rip van Winkle walked slowly through the village he saw many new, grand houses. There were streets where he remembered fields had been. There were more people, too, but still not one he knew; even the dogs were strangers.

As he walked people stared at him and seemed amused; children pointed at him rudely and followed him through the streets. Men stopped their work to watch him. He asked one of them the way to his house, bracing himself for the terrible fury of his wife – but when he reached the gate he saw the house was in ruins, the roof fallen in and the windows broken. What had happened? Where were his wife and family? As he went sadly on his way he caught sight of an old man in a shop window staring at him. Rip waved to the stranger, then realized . . . the old, old man with tattered hat and long, white beard was himself! No wonder the village folk had stared!

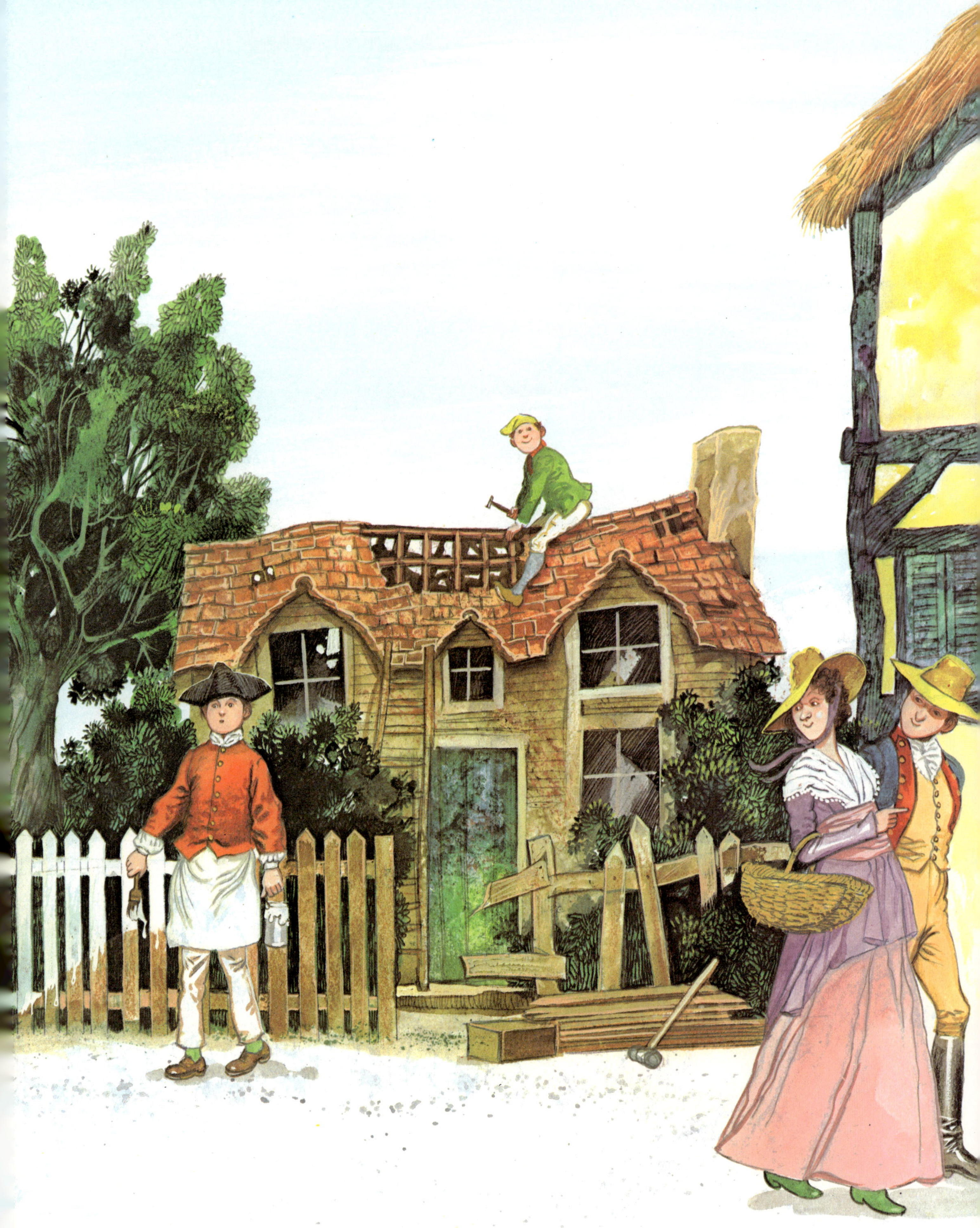

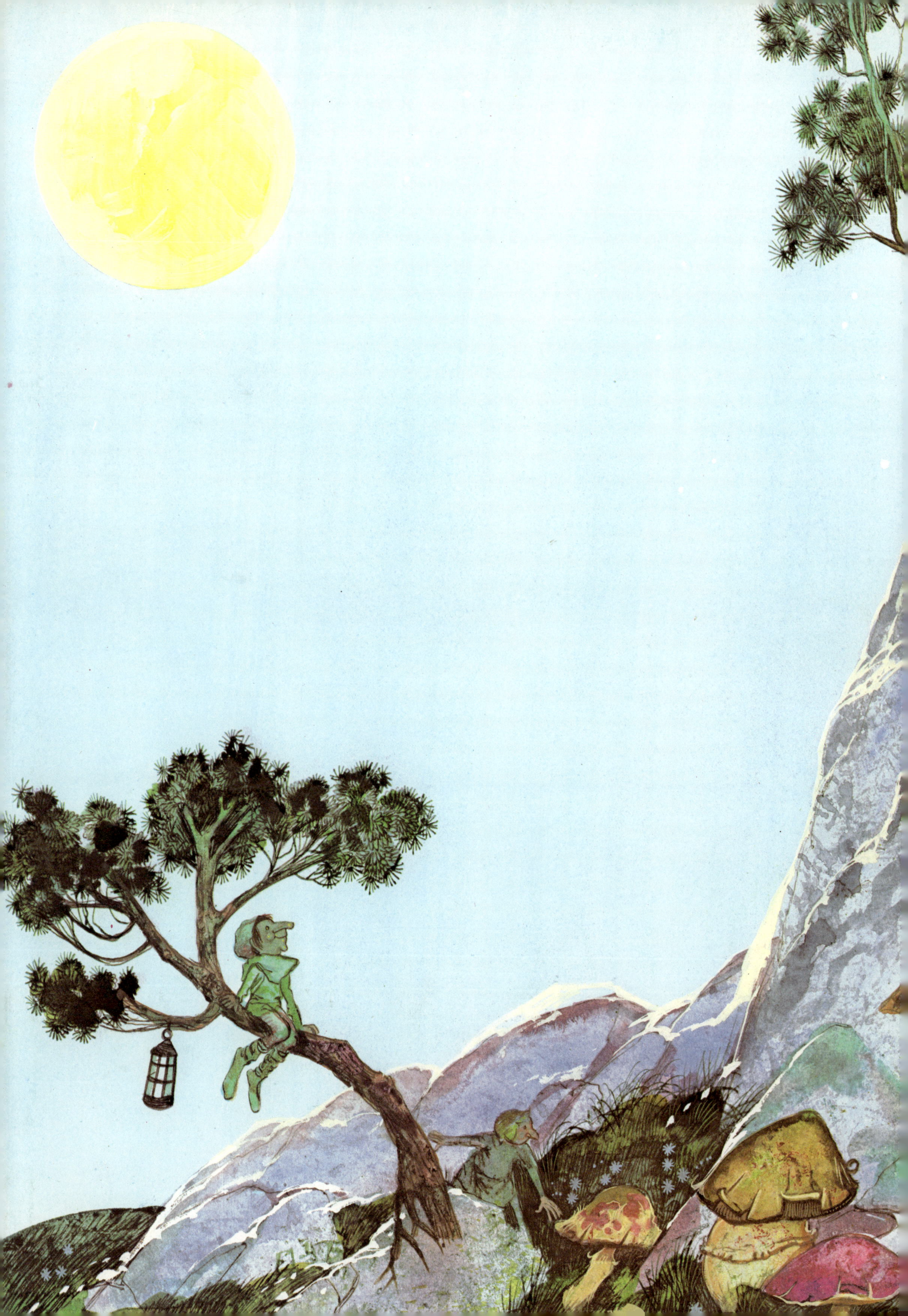